Forbidden Love

A prequel to No Turning Back

KAREN WEAVER

First published by Making Magic Happen Academy, 2017
Copyright © 2017 Karen Weaver
Edited by Teena Raffa-Mulligan

National Library of Australia
Cataloguing-in-Publication data:
Forbidden Love/ Karen Weaver
ISBN: (sc) 978-0-6480432-5-6
ISBN: (e) 978-0-6480432-6-3
Romance – fiction

Making Magic Happen Academy books may be ordered through online booksellers or by contacting:
www.makingmagichappenacademy.com

Forbidden Love

'So, it's really happening, Sarah' Jade turns to face her best friend.

'Yes, it is.' Sarah eases back into the wicker chair located on the sunset-facing verandah of her childhood home.

'To think that this time six months ago we were partying in the city, and now we are back home the night before your wedding.'

'Life can take unexpected turns.' There is a smile in Sarah's voice.

'Oh, your beloved optimism.' Jade peers into the distance as the sun sets over the treetops.

'I'm fine with it all, Jade, please don't worry for me.'

'Well, you have been with Danny for years.'

'That I have.'

'And to think that in a few months you'll be a mum as well as a wife.

'I'm so scared and excited.'

'You will be the best mum.'

'I suppose we have to grow up some time, don't we?'

'Really?' Jade laughs. 'I am not planning on it anytime soon.' She raises her glass of rose wine.

'A toast. To my beautiful forever friend and the beautiful little family she is creating.'

Suddenly she bursts into tears and buries her face in both hands.

Sarah reaches for her, full of concern. 'Jade, what's up?'

'What am I supposed to do without you? You keep me on the right track. Even dancing won't be the same without you by my side. We've never been apart and you have to go and grow up.'

Sarah gives her friend's hand a reassuring squeeze. 'You'll fall in love too, Jade.'

Jade doesn't think so. Not if past experience is anything to go by. She fumbles in her pocket for a tissue to dry her eyes.

Danny emerges from inside the house. 'Haven't you two done enough catching up? I'm missing my bride-to-be.'

Sarah giggles. 'I've only been gone twenty minutes.'

He leans over and gives her a lingering kiss. She rises and stands snuggled against him. The two of them seem embraced by their love. It's too much for Jade and she cannot watch, turning her attention to the distant trees, the fading sky. A thread of jealousy weaves through her and she pushes it away.

This is her best friend. She wants her to be happy, of course she does. They have been together throughout their schooldays, rarely apart even when they went on to study dance and toured with a cast of Irish dancers taking Ireland by storm.

It's tough to accept that Sarah has suddenly been shuffled down a different road to the one she is walking. Jade shakes her head. Only two months ago they were a dynamic duo (well trio if you include Sarah's high school sweetheart, Danny Jenkins) partying hard in the city, living life to the full. Now in a blink of an eye Jade feels like she's lost her best friend as Sarah's family have taken over her life and arranged this shotgun wedding. Danny is Sarah's forever love, Jade can see that, but what does that mean for their friendship? It's going to change and she's not ready for that. She'll miss Sarah so much. There's a magic about her and Jade wants to hold on to that but already she can feel the difference in their relationship. Sarah always says the universe works in mysterious ways. Maybe it's time she embraced that philosophy too.

Jade slips quietly away, certain the happy couple don't even notice her leaving. Deep in thought, she enters the grand front entrance of Sarah's family home, almost colliding with someone about to exit.

'Oi!'

Jade freezes. She knows that voice. 'Cath?' It's the last person she'd expect to see at Sarah and Danny's wedding.

'Jade, you ole slapper, how the hell are ya?'

'I'm good, how are you?' It doesn't come easily, but she's polite.

'Never been better, hon.'

'I didn't know you were going to be here.' What she really wants to say is, 'Go. Now. You are not wanted here.'

'Sure wasn't I one of Sarah's best friends in school so her mum's asked me to be a bridesmaid.'

A shiver runs up Jade's spine. Cath a bridesmaid? The woman who tried to steal Danny from Sarah, who almost ruined her life? 'Uh … does Sarah know about this?'

Cath grins. 'Nah, her mum said it would be a nice surprise. She's organised the dress and all.'

Jade catches her breath. Surpise, no. Shock, yes. What was Mrs Banks thinking?

Cath is still speaking. 'So where is the slapper? I hear she's knocked up.'

'She's resting. So where are you staying, Cath?'

'We have a room here tonight. Tomorrow is going to be a blast huh. We can have a right ole session.'

'It will be a magical day,' Jade replies. *I hope* remains unspoken.

'It'll be a good ole knees up…'

Jade's attention is no longer on their conversation. Her gaze is fixed on the rugged blond man approaching. Her heart does a somersault. That's never happened before.

'Who's that?' she asks, finding her voice.

'Keep your sticky paws off him, Jade,' warns Cath. She walks off waving, 'Over here, hon,' giving Jade one last piercing dagger look over her shoulder.

With Cath clinging to his arm, Mr Rugged Blond returns Jade's glance. Her heart is racing and every cell in her body feels alert. No stranger has ever caused such a reaction. This wedding has just become a lot more interesting.

*****

Next morning Jade is up from cock crow, thanks to the hens and roosters located right outside her bedroom window. She pops on her running gear and makes her way out of the house. The tree-lined drive makes for easy enjoyable running. Daffodils have popped up in scattered clumps around the magnificent evergreen trees that guard the grand stone residence. She steers off the main track, navigating down a path that leads to a lake. The combination of water, trees and the fresh morning air awakens her inner core in the most harmonising way. She stops to stretch out her body and watch the land awaken before her eyes, tantalised by the array of colours and textures that paint a picture in the sky. Breathing deeply, she reflects on how many people miss these magical moments most people miss as they slumber soundly, not yet ready to begin their day.

Suddenly she tenses. Someone is watching her. She looks around, but there is no one to be seen. After a few more stretches she begins to make her way back to the house so that the magnificent craziness of Sarah's big day can commence. This day is so special for her best friend. *Nothing can go wrong.* She won't let it.

Picking up pace as she strides along the path edging the lake, a mother duck and her ducklings catch her eye. It's a mistake, for she fails to notice the damage in the path ahead and next thing she knows she has toppled sideways and landed head first in a bush.

'You okay?' The voice is strong and masculine, the accent distinctly Australian.

Jade tries to dislodge herself from her bottom up position. *Jesus Christ could this be any more embarrassing?* Two strong arms dislodge her from the bush and set her back on her feet. But he doesn't release her, continuing to hold her steady. Heat floods her face. She's sure her hair must resemble the bush he just extracted her from. He is looking into her eyes, searching her soul. It doesn't make sense but she wants to melt into his embrace. The urge to kiss him is intense. Tingles ripple through her. Jade leans closer. Closer. His rugged maleness is almost overpowering. His arms around her feel so right…

Snap! The sound startles Jade back to reality and she quickly steps back with an embarrassed cough and disengages from his embrace. He laughs softly.

'Where were you Brax?' It's Cath, reclaiming her man.

Jade strides quickly away, giving herself a sound talking to. *What was she thinking? This man is totally out of bounds. She has no business feeling an attraction for him. She has to stop it. Now.*

***

Jade tries to stay focused, refusing to allow thoughts of the rugged Australian to enter her mind.

It's her best friend's wedding day and even though it is a shotgun wedding there has been no expense spared for the daughter of big shot hotel owner Gerald Banks. Extravagence is his trademark. His home is big and bold in design and his children have always had the best of the best. Sarah's 'situation' is a closely guarded secret around town and anyone who let it slip would not easily be forgiven.

Jade loves the dress Sarah has chosen for her bridesmaids. Strapless, with a golden love heart bustier and a fitted long gold matte satin skirt, it complements Jade's figure and colouring. She feels a little sorry for Sarah's chubby cousin Denise. The dress is less flattering for her. Sarah's third bridesmaid, Lucy, is a bit of a mystery. Jade doesn't know her well. She's very young and has only entered Sarah's life in the past year and no one is disclosing any information about who she is or where she came from. Cath's presence in the bridal party is an even bigger mystery. What a strange thing for Mrs Banks to do, arranging a surprise bridesmaid. She's such a gentle soul who loves everyone and everything with an open heart. She must have recalled Cath being around the girls throughout their school years without knowing the details of how she tormented them all at school.

Sarah's arrival interrupts Jade's musings, and she isn't alone in the thrill that fills her at the sight of her friend. There is a chorus of oohs and aahs. Sarah's dress is breathtaking, a halter neck satin gown with white pearls decorating the neckline and gathered in clusters all over the fabric. It is truly complimentary to her beautiful figure and there's no sign of baby bump.

'You all look lovely,' she says and opens her arms for them all to huddle hug. But as they break away, she whispers to Jade, 'I can't believe she's here.'

'Today is about you Sarah, and you look amazing. Look at you.' Jade swooshes her friend over to the full-length mirror in the corner of the room where the sun shines through the magnificent floor-to- ceiling bay windows.

'I do, don't I?' she beams.

There is a light tap at the door and Mrs Banks peeps in. Sarah looks away. Jade catches the brief flicker of anger that crosses her friend's face. So they've had words about Cath.

'How are we all?' sings Mrs Banks. 'Don't you all look a picture.' She casts a cautious glance at her daughter. 'And look at you. You are a princess. Happy?'

'Yes, very happy.'

'Then let's do this. Your car is outside.'

Mr Banks is waiting at the bottom of the staircase and his eyes light up when he sees his daughter. Jade feels a pang and blinks back the threatened tears. How wonderful it must be to have a father's love. She's never known that. But this is not the time for regrets and if only. This is Sarah's day and nothing must spoil it. She carefully carries Sarah's lace trail and they carefully descend one step at a time. Every treasured moment is being filmed. On reaching the bottom, Sarah takes her father's hand. He kisses it and tenderly looks towards her. 'You look beautiful, my dear.'

Sarah smiles and continues to walk hand in hand with her dad towards the front entrance. A white Bentley awaits them beyond the hand-carved double entrance doors.

Sarah can no longer fight back the tears. 'You did this for me?'

'Of course, my dear, you deserve the best.'

'But I have let you down, Dad.'

'Nonsense child, you have lifted me up.'

'Oh, my make-up,' she giggles, as they compose themselves.

Mr Banks turns and glares at Jade as if to say, *Why are you not onto this situation?*

With fumbling fingers, she quickly takes a compact from her clutch bag and repairs Sarah's make up.

The bride's car heads for Crom Castle and the romantic ceremony of Sarah's dreams, the bridesmaids following closely in a matching white car. Even from her seat in the front, Jade can feel Cath's animosity boring into her from the back seat of the vehicle. Unease grips her. Such venom cannot possibly attract a positive outcome. And she's done nothing. Nothing. She didn't plan to fall face first into a bush just as Cath's man was passing by.

They have reached the castle gatehouse. The small old stone building has housed the guardian of the castle for centuries. The gates now remain open to welcome visitors, but this was not always the case. The laneway is long and surrounded by a vast breathtaking green landscape that is home to many of nature's animals. Deer can often be seen in the meadows, though they shy away from human contact.

Despite her best intentions, Jade's thoughts return to that moment with Brax, that almost kiss. She blushes as a surge of emotion rushes through her and she yearns for that feeling again.

In an attempt to refocus she observes the vastness of fields and the tree-lined laneway as they enter the private grounds of the castle. There on a hill the most magnificent building appears before them. The large wooden door opens and the Earl appears to welcome the bride. She has been granted permission to enter from the private castle entrance, enabling her to arrive with minimal detection from the groom's party.

The large arched pine doors at the end of the long elegant hallway open to a grand L-shaped conservatory. A flood of light bursts through. Music begins, a cue for the wedding parade. Gasps fill the room as Sarah makes her way to the love of her life standing in a demure suit at the top of the aisle.

As if of their own accord, Jade's eyes find Brax's among the gathering. With difficulty and a helpful nudge from one of the bridesmaids, she returns her focus to what is required of the chief bridesmaid. But as she follows Sarah down the aisle, her thoughts continue to wander. She is intensely aware of the rugged Australian. . *Stop it, stop it, stop it!* she tells herself until she realises his eyes are meeting hers look for look. The memory of the way he sensed her inner desires this morning sears through her, sending a flush to her face and the shiver of goosebumps all over her skin. Everyone will notice. Cath will notice.

She drags her gaze from his, concentrates on walking slowly and attentively behind Sarah and her dad. A sudden sharp nudge in her back unsteadies her balance and in the nick of time she regains control. Oh yes. Cath witnessed her boyfriend looking at another woman when he should have been looking at her. That has got to hurt. Jade catches a breath. *What is that? Surely not empathy for Cath?*

'You may kiss the bride.'

The ceremony is over. At last Jade can melt into the background, try to make sense of this ridiculous attraction for Brax.

***

The hall has gone quiet and the dance floor has cleared. Sarah grabs Jade by both arms.

'Jade, my most beautiful friend, it is time for us to dance together.'

'What?'

Sarah alters her wedding dress by pulling off half her skirt to reveal she is wearing white lace pumps. She giggles. 'Clever, hey? Your dress does this too.'

'You're kidding me.'

'No. And here are some gold pumps for you.'

Jade beams as she transitions from bridesmaid to performer. Irish dancing is the only place in the world where she feels no restraint. In no time she joins her best friend on the dance floor.

'Happy?' asks Sarah.

'Hell yes, I'm happy.'

Sarah claps her hands and melodic Celtic music begins. The crowd joins in with a unified clapping rhythm.

They flow in and out of steps effortlessly. They are magical together; every time they dance it is special and today more so than ever. Every leg stretched is executed with such precision, every step is in unison. It's as if they share the same heartbeat, the same shadow. This is what they have lived for. The final few steps are dramatic, ending with strong pointed toes and long straight bodies.

The crowd cheers. The girls laugh and hug each other tightly.

'Thank you,' Jade whispers.

Sarah smiles. 'Until we dance again. I love you, Jade.'

'I am so happy to see you so happy.'

Danny comes to share the moment and hugs his new bride. He kisses her gently, his hand joining hers on their little bump.

'You know this means you've got to grow up now, Danny,' Jade teases.

'Ah, my wife will keep me on track, Jadey. You may have to do some growing up yourself.'

He's right. She's going to miss Sarah's guidance. Sarah is now the one who needs support and Danny has put his hand up for that job. Tears fill her eyes and she brushes them away with her fingers, careful not to smudge her makeup.

Danny pats her on the shoulder. 'Sorry, I didn't mean to make you cry.'

'No, it's okay, Dan, I am just going to miss you guys.'

'But we are not going anywhere,' says Sarah.

'No, I know, but… things will change and you won't need me hanging off you.'

'This little one will need an aunty.'

Smiling, Jade hugs them both. 'I love you two. I'll be fine. It's your special day, let's enjoy it.'

Something catches Jade's attention. It's Cath. She has come running into the reception area without Brax. Her eyes are red and she is hugging her mum.

Does this mean?

Brax is next to return. He looks at Cath with a sorry glance and then begins scouring the room. His glance fixes on Jade. This does not go unnoticed by the crowd. She wants to crawl under a rock but there is nowhere to hide. Brax is striding towards her with intent, Cath storming behind him with a face of thunder.

'Jade, can we chat?' His voice is a caress.

'Erm…I don't think so.' Jade nods to the force beyond him.

He turns and Cath lifts her fist and punches him on the nose. 'I hope that you two will be very happy together. Not!'

Brax touches his nose. A trickle of blood dribbles onto his shirt.

'Are you okay?' Jade doesn't feel okay. Her legs are wobbly and her hand is shaking as she searches in her clutch purse for a tissue to tend to his bleeding.

'Yeah, sure, no worries there.'

He does look more surprised than hurt.

'Umm…'

She is interrupted by someone grabbing her arm and dragging her away to a corner.

'Jade Alexandra what in goodness name do you think you are doing?'

'Mum.'

'Yes, dear child, do you not know what you are getting mixed up with?'

'You mean me and…?'

'Yes, you and that lad.'

Jade looks around to see Brax being escorted out of the castle by a fuming Mr Banks and one of his friends.

'Mum, I haven't done anything wrong.'

'It doesn't look that way, everyone is talking about it. Stealing your friend's boyfriend. You do know that he is supposed to be the dad of Sheila Graham's baby too.'

'You've got it all wrong.'

'Maybe I have but I don't want you having anything to do with him. No good could come of it. Understand?'

There's concern behind the anger in her mother's eyes. Jade sighs. Even though she's never met a man who stirred so much emotion in her, it's not worth the hassle. She's barely met him and already he's caused trouble. Best to walk away, not get involved.

'Yes, Mum. I do understand.'

'Good.' Her mum's demeanor relaxes immediately. Seeing how deflated Jade is she places her hand on her cheek. 'Love, it's for the best and look at Sean, he can't take his eyes off you. Now that would be a good lad to allow into your heart, Jade.'

Jade gives her mum a *Don't go there* stare.

'You and Sarah danced beautifully together.'

'Thanks, Mum.' Sarah is trying to grab her attention with an *I'll meet you in the toilets* mime. 'Mum, I've got to go check on Sarah.'

'Okay, love.'

En route she is confronted by someone she really does not want to see right now. Sarah's dad.

'Young lady, you have not only been the most incompetent chief bridesmaid, you have created a scene. Do you know how much we have put into this day? Only for you to come along and single-handedly ruin it.'

'I'm sorry, Mr Banks, I never…'

He cuts her off before she can offer any explanation.

'I think that it might be a good idea for you to leave right now, maybe then we can enjoy the rest of the day without drama.'

'But Mr Banks, I have to check on…'

'I asked you to leave.' He stands firm.

First my own mother has a go and now Mr Banks is throwing me out. Could this day get any worse? Oh yes, and my best friend is waiting for me in the toilets.

Jade feels she has no choice but to leave. The darkness meets her as she leaves the grand conservatory, eerily haunting her to the core.

What am I going to do?

She pulls out her phone to call a taxi.

'…Oh. Really that long? Yes, I will wait.'

Jade wraps both hands around herself. Should she go back inside? She really needs to check on Sarah. Maybe Mr Banks has had some time to calm down. Music filters out from the glowing conservatory. It's the slow first dance for the bride and groom. Jade watches through the window and is relieved to see her friend creating a treasured memory dancing with Danny.

'Destiny is at work you know.'

The familiar voice startles Jade. His voice is low and charismatic.

'Really, what makes you say that?'

As he moves closer to her, his chest brushes against hers. The masculine smell of him takes her breath away., making her feel light-headed and floaty.

'You can't tell me that you don't feel it too.'

He lifts her arms and places them around his neck. She cannot resist, melting instead into his embrace. Together, they dance in the moonlight, a slow, sensual duet.

The glow from the wedding reception provides light, just enough for her to see an outline of his face. She can't help looking into his whirlpool eyes, his lips inviting her lower. She resists, he doesn't. The sensitivity of his caressing kiss romances her soul. It touches her deepest being. All rational thoughts vacate her mind mind as she gives way to the moment, embracing every head to toe tingle.

Moving to the rhythm of the slow song playing indoors, they swoon across the grass. His dance skills surprise her as she is swept off her feet literally and metaphorically.

The darkness of the night is interrupted by headlights making their way up the lengthy driveway.

'That will be my taxi,' she breathes against his chest.

'You can't go.' His voice is low and husky. 'Stay with me tonight.'

'That's not a good idea.'

'Why? Do you not want to?'

His tone makes her soft – something she is not used to being. He kisses her neck.

'Stay with me.'

She is a servant to his words. 'Okay.'

Taking her by the hand he leads her to the edge of the forest. 'Let's hide.'

They duck down, watching as the taxi pulls up to the castle and the driver beeps the horn.

'I feel bad,' whispers Jade.

Brax laughs. 'Why? It's just a taxi driver.'

'But he's waiting there for me and he could be on another job.'

'You're cute.'

They watch as the taxi driver gets out of the car and goes into the venue.

'Now, where were we?' Brax pulls her closer – she's putty in his hands.

She is distracted by muffled voices outside the castle. It's the taxi driver with three new passengers.

'See, I told you it would be okay.'

Jade giggles. 'No you didn't.'

'Well I was meant to.'

They both laugh together.

'Ssh, they're coming, hide.'

The lights of the car go past and Brax pulls her up into his arms. 'Let's go.'

'Where are we going?'

'You'll see.'

They walk hand and hand in the darkness down the long lane with only moonlight illuminating their path.

'There's no way I would do this on my own,' she confides.

'Wouldn't you? Do I make you feel safe then?'

'I think that you do.'

He holds her hand tighter as they take a right turn, heading off the straight path.

'Why are we going down here? This is the way to the visitor centre.'

'You'll see.'

'Okay.'

But is it? A whisper of doubt creeps in. This guy could be a serial killer and she has placed herself in the perfect position of being his next target. She's not the best judge of character.

'Don't worry, I'm not some sort of serial killer or anything.'

OMG did he just read my mind! 'Well that's a relief.'

He laughs.

I am willing to take my chances on Brax rather than go it alone in this vast darkness. It's the longest unnerving ten minutes of her life. Every time an animal moves in the surrounding fields or an owl hoots, she jumps into his arms. *Maybe he is staying in one of the cottages, yes that has to be it.*

Her relief is short-lived for when they reach the centre he walks past the cottages. *Oh God.* What has she got herself into? She must plan her escape.

'This way,' he says and leads her round a corner and there's the jetty. 'See, isn't she a beaut?'

She punches him on the shoulder.

'Hey, what's that for?'

'You could have told me where we were going. My mind was racing in every direction.'

'I wanted to surprise you.'

'You have.' It sounds annoyed rather than pleased, but she can't help that.

'Don't be like that, I promise she is beautiful and unique, just like you.'

She softens as they stroll down to the lit-up jetty. Moonlight shimmers on the water. A houseboat filled with character is moored at the end of the jetty.

This could be fun.

'Isn't she gorgeous?' The pride in his voice is obvious.

'Is she yours?'

'She is for now. Come on, let me introduce you to Bessie.'

Inside, the boat is neat and cosy.

'Make yourself comfy. I'll get us a drink.'

Being with Brax is intriguing. Jade senses his zest for life and it excites her. Everyone around her has always guided her to play it safe, not take risks in fear of failing. She is finished with not following her heart. It's not the ideal scenario to start a relationship, going off with another woman's boyfriend at her best friend's wedding. It's so completely out of character for her. But how can she ignore the way Brax makes her feel? His very presence makes her stomach flutter and when he touches her, every hair stands on end. He makes her feel alive, and this feeling has been dormant for way too long.

The night slips away in conversation and getting to know each other. Never before has she succumbed to the temptation of a man on the first night, but how can she resist Brax? She feels connected to him on so many levels, not just physically. Though he certainly has a lot to offer in that department with his firm, muscular body and defined six-pack. Jade smiles to herself as she watches him slip out of his shirt. Her mum would never give her blessing to what she's about to do but Jade can only listen to her heart in this moment. And while everyone else in her life might warn her 'No!', her heart is clearly saying, 'Yes!'

When Jade wakes, Brax is gone. There's no answer when she calls him, so she wraps a sheet around herself and explores the boat but there's no sign of him. Has he left her here? Just like that?. She begins to dress and tenses as heavy footsteps approach on the jetty. She watches the hatch doors, every muscle taut. Is it him? It could be anyone. She is here on her own.

When the hatch slowly opens and Brax lowers himself in, she releases her breath in a whoosh of relief.

'You okay, babe? I went to get us breakfast at the café.'

'That's great, thank you.'

'I didn't want to wake you, you looked so peaceful.' He snuggles up beside her. His eyes are blue and dreamy. 'Do you want to grab some fresh air out on the deck before we set sail?'

'Set sail?'

'Yeah, I thought we could spend the day on the water. It's real beaut out there today.'

There's nothing Jade would like more. Brax makes her feel good and if she goes home her mum will be on her case for leaving the way she did. A day avoiding the confrontation that most certainly awaits her is an excellent idea.

'That sounds lovely.'

They make their way up the three wooden steps to the deck. The sun has risen and shades of orange are a backdrop to the pink clouds.

'That's magical,' sighs Jade, leaning against him.

'Yes, and look how it glows on the water.'

He appreciates the elements of nature. Impressive.

'You being here to share it with me makes it more special,' he says quietly.

Jade flushes. 'I bet you say that to all the girls.'

He smiles, but doesn't take the bait.

'Hey, did you know that the saying is *Pink sky at night, shepherd's delight; pink sky in the morning, shepherd's warning?*'

'So you're being warned, hey?'

'Maybe,' she teases.

He wraps his arms around her and she nestles into him. Later, looking out over the water and eating croissants, Jade can't think of anywhere she would rather be in this moment. A surprise bucket list item. It's like being in a different world, here on the houseboat with Brax, a world without cares, where Jade doesn't have to worry about anything. So simple and fulfilling.

They spend the day exploring the waterways. Jade has lived not far from this area all her life yet she had never experienced it from this perspective.

She even catches her first fish, another exhilarating bucket list moment she never knew she wanted.

'You love the water, don't you Brax?'

'Yeah, there's something about it that calls me. It's so safe over here though. In Australia there are more things to be careful of. Here you can just set off.'

'What like?'

'Aw it depends where you are but in the sea you've got those darn sharks to watch out for, stingrays, and killer jellyfish.'

Jade can't hide her horror and he shakes his head.

'It's not that bad. You just have to respect their environment and be aware.'

'Oh okay,, well that's all right then,' she laughs.

'What do you do for fun?'

'I dance.'

'I saw you dance at the wedding. That's awesome stuff.'

'Yes but it's not going to be the same without Sarah.'

'Why not?'

'We've always danced together. We've been on auditions together, worked together and practically been inseparable since birth.'

'Woah, that's pretty full on.'

'Yeah I know, but she is having a baby and just got married so everything is changing.'

'A change can be a good thing.'

'You reckon?'

She lowers her head. He places his fingers gently on her chin and raises her face to look at him.

'If it hadn't been for this change you wouldn't be sitting here with me right now, would you?'

'No, you're right. I have space in my life for new things now.'

'Yes, it's exciting, not depressing.'

His words nurture her worries away.

'Hey you never know, you may even come back to Oz with me.'

'Let's take it one step at a time.'

'The sun will be going down soon so we had better moor somewhere. I know the perfect place.'

'I'd best be getting back, my mum will be worried.'

'Just one more night?' He holds her close and rests his head on hers, his breath in her hair.

How can she resist? 'Okay, but I will have to phone my mum. Where are we mooring?'

'It's not far away.'

They sail past an island with a perimeter of trees. The sky entertains again with oranges and pinks.

'*Pink sky at night, shepherd's delight,*' Brax teases.

'Well that sounds promising,' she teases back.

Then there it is, a thatched cottage on the water's edge. Not just any Irish cottage, but a large restaurant.

'It's a treasure, isn't it?' he says with a smile.

'Yes, it is.'

They walk hand in hand along the jetty, the chill of the night drawing them closer together for warmth, the smell of soulful food wafting invitingly on the air.

A glow of warmth and laughter draws them inside where red brick walls and oak furniture add to the warm ambience.

'Welcome, welcome, come on in,' a short bubbly Frenchman greets them and ushers them to a fireside table for two. The pointed tips of his moustache rise up to tickle his rosy cheeks.

'See anything you want?' Jade asks when the menus arrive.

'Yes, I see exactly what I want, but it's not on this menu.'

'Oh smooth.'

'I like to think so,' he laughs.

Once their orders are placed for a Caesar salad for her and a steak for him, Brax scans the room until he spots a TV broadcasting football results.

'You like sports then,' she says.

'Yes and I'm keen to watch one of your Gaelic football matches.'

'The All-Ireland semi-finals are held in my hometown every year. Maybe we could go together.'

He doesn't hesitate. 'That sounds like a plan.'

'Great.'

Something has shifted between them. Their hands meet across the table and the sensation is electric. As they smile into each other's eyes, Jade has never felt such a sense of rightness about them being together.

'I like spending time with you, Brax, it makes me feel good.'

He squeezes her hand tight and leans towards her. "Jade, I…'

The demanding ringing of her cell phone interrupts.

She quickly checks the caller ID. 'I had better get this. It's Mum. Hello—what?'

Jade feels the blood draining from her face

'Okay, I'll be right there.'

She ends the call and begins frantically getting her things together. 'I've got to go. It's Sarah, she needs me.'

She practically runs out of the restaurant but is still waiting outside when he emerges after paying the bill.

He places his hands on her waist and tries to draw her close but she pulls away, refusing to respond, even to look at him.

'What's wrong?'

'It's my fault. I shouldn't have gone with you. It was the wrong thing to do.'

'Why? Didn't you enjoy yourself? You seemed really happy.'

'Yes, but that doesn't make it right. I am hurting too many people.'

'Jade, it is okay to be happy you know.'

She doesn't respond.

Beyond the perimeter of the restaurant it is pitch black. The darkness is soon pierced by a bright light and loud engine noise approaches. A black motorbike pulls up and the rider hands Jade a helmet.

She puts it on and hops on the back. Before pulling down the visor she looks at Brax. Her heart lurches. He looks so rugged and handsome. She wants him in a way she has never wanted anyone. But she must not give in. Their eyes meet for a moment before she flips her visor and taps the rider to go. Every shred of her being is urging her to look back. It is such an effort to resist. And as the bike speeds through the night, Jade realises this is a theme in her life, resisting her desires to please others rather than herself.

When they arrive at the hospital, Jade's thoughts are in turmoil. One scenario after another plays out, each one worse than the last. Her mother didn't go into detail, just said Sarah was in the hospital and to get to the pediatric ward as soon as she could.

Dear Lord, please let her be okay, dear Lord, please let her be okay. She recites the prayer every step of the way.

Arriving at the ward she presses the buzzer to enter and waits until a nurse arrives to ask her business and admit her.

But as she approaches Ward Three, Jade can't shake the shame that is weighing her down. Whatever has happened, she wasn't there for Sarah. She has let her down in the worst possible way. On passing a mirror she catches a glimpse of herself. Her hair is a mess and she is wearing Brax's denim jacket over her bridesmaid dress. But it doesn't matter how she looks. All that matters is Sarah. She holds her breath as she pushes open the door to the ward, and exhales with relief at the sight of Sarah and Danny. *Best case scenario.*

'Where have you been?' The blast from Danny is totally out of character. He's usually so laid back.

Jade falters, taken aback. 'Mmm—'

'Danny, it's okay, she's here now,' Sarah says quietly from her bed. 'Are you okay, Jade?'

Jade bursts into tears. Typical Sarah to worry about her best friend, when she is pale and weak, with eyes red-rimmed from crying.

'Danny, why don't you go get something to eat,' Sarah suggest.

His lips are a thin line as he glares at Jade. 'No, I think I'll stay.'

'Danny, please, Jade and I need a few moments.'

'Well − okay.' He goes over and kisses Sarah's hand, murmurs softly, 'I won't be long.'

As he leaves the room, he warns, 'Don't upset her.'

Jade nods. What sort of friend does he think she is? Of course she knows the answer to that and holds in a sob.

Sarah beckons her over to the bed.

'Is it the baby?' Jade hardly dares to ask. She knows how wanted it was even though the pregnancy was unplanned.

Sarah's face crumples and she can't speak for the tears, but only nod.

'Oh no.' Jade folds her friend in her arms and they cling together, sobbing.

A cough alerts them that Danny has returned.

'The doctors say that they need to talk to us.'

'I'll go.'

Jade goes to stand but Sarah clutches at her hand.

'No, please stay, that's okay isn't it, Danny?'

He looks from one to the other before nodding briefly.

A team of doctors enters the ward and Sarah's grip tightens on Jade's hand as they wait to hear what urgent news has brought them here.

'I have been checking over your ultrasounds,' announces the specialist after introducing himself as Dr Rashid. 'We would like to schedule in another as soon as possible to confirm it, but there appears to be a second fetus.'

Danny voice trembles with emotion. 'We are still having a baby?'

'Yes,' smiles Dr Rashid. 'We suspect you have had a multiple pregnancy and now have a single pregnancy.'

Jade watches as the pain turns to hope for her two dearest friends. Sarah is so overwhelmed she can't find the words, but she does retrieve her hands from their grasp and place them on her abdomen. Jade doesn't quite catch her whispered message to the little one who survived.

The specialist takes on a stern expression. 'I cannot stress enough the need for rest. You are still in the risk zone. We will monitor you over the next few days and reassess you for discharge then.'

'I will stay with her and make sure she rests,' Danny says.

Sarah breaks her silence. 'Thank you, doctor.'

It takes a few moments after the doctors leave for the reality of the situation to sink in.

Jade feels like her smile is a mile wide. 'This is good news. I am so happy for you both.'

'Pass me my phone, Dan, I have to call our mums.'

Danny pushes her gently down on the pillows. 'No, I'll do it. You have to rest.'

'And I must leave you to it.' Jade stands to go. 'I need to call my mum too.'

'Yes, she's worried about you, where were you?'

'Ah Sarah, don't be worrying about that now, you need to focus on you and your baby.'

Sarah gives her the *I want to know now* look.

'I'll tell you another time, okay? I'm going to go and face the music.'

'Remember it's only because your mum cares so much.'

'Yes, I know.' She hugs her friend and fist pumps Danny.

'Hey I'm sorry about...you know,' Danny apologises.

'All cool, Danny.'

The sense of relief leaving is a total contrast to the anxiety she felt arriving. Jade is so grateful that for now, all is well. 'Thank you' she quietly whispers to the sky.

It's been a long a day for Jade and all she wants to do on arriving home is have a shower and snuggle up with a good book. When she enters the front door after paying the taxi, her mother is sitting in the living room stitching a design onto a handkerchief. With a bit of luck she might be able to slip upstairs to her room without an interrogation.

'Come here, darling.'

'I'm just going to have a shower Mum.'

'Jade.'

There is no ignoring that tone of command. Jade sighs. All she wants is to wash the past 48 hours down the drain but it isn't going to happen yet. She changes direction and takes a seat opposite her mother in the cosy room warmed by the glow of a blazing fire.

Her mother sets aside her embroidery and pins Jade with a look she knows all too well.

'I would like to know where you have been for the past two days, though I suspect that you will be reluctant to share that, and so I want you to listen to me. When I was a little younger than you I fell for a handsome fun guy who made me feel good. I did things that were out of character for me and I paid the price.'

'Mum, I am not you.'

'But my dear, you are more like me than you could ever know.'

'Mum, I'm tired and hungry and I need a shower. If you have anything else to say it will have to wait.'

Jade doesn't wait for a reply. In no mood for a lecture, she leaps up from the chair and strides purposefully out of the room.

A shower and a change of clothes makes her feel half-way human once more and she heads to the kitchen. Her mother is already there and has a sandwich and a cup of tea waiting for her. Jade mumbles her thanks.

'I had a visitor this evening,' says her mother, leaning against the breakfast bar.

Jade looks up. 'Visitor?'

'Yes, Sean O'Driscoll popped by.'

'Oh. Him.' Jade opens her sandwich and carefully removes the cucumber.

'Jade, he's a perfect match for you, he's such a talented young man with so many prospects for the future. I've seen you dance together, you have chemistry.'

Jade almost chokes on a bite of her chicken and salad sandwich. She swallows, shaking her head. 'Mum, you have got it all wrong. That is not good chemistry we have going on. He's a sleaze.'

'He really likes you and wants to show you you're right for each other. Just give him a chance when he calls back around tonight.'

'What? I don't want to see him, he's not my type.'

'The Australian gypsy is then?'

'I have more chemistry with him if that's what you're implying.'

'I don't want you to see him again, Jade, he is not good for you or your career.'

'Mum, I'm twenty-three years old. You can't tell me who I can or cannot see.'

'No, but you still need guidance. I wish someone had cared enough to guide me when I was your age.'

Right. The blossoming stage career swept away overnight due to an unexpected pregnancy. Jade knows that story. She's been hearing it since childhood.

'Can we stop talking about it now, please? I'm just back from seeing Sarah and I would have thought how she is was more important than my love life.'

Eleanor sits at the table and reaches across to take Jade's hand. 'I'm sorry. Of course. I've just been worrying about you. How is the beautiful girl?'

'She is so strong, Mum. I would love to be that strong. She was told that she had lost the baby and then they found out she was still pregnant with a second baby but still at risk. Mum, it's all my fault.'

Jade bursts into tears. Instantly her mother is out of her chair and around the table, giving her daughter a much-needed hug.

'It's not your fault, darling. How can it be?'

'It is, Mum, I make stupid choices. Why can't I do the right thing? What is wrong with me?'

'There's nothing wrong with you, darling.'

'Then why do I always get it so wrong? Look at Brax, he's not the best choice but my heart screams *Go for it*. Why? Why can't I say No?'

'It's not that it is wrong, darling, it is just that you can't see what others can see because you are blinded by lust.'

'I know it's wrong, Mum, but it feels so right.'

'I know, Jade and I have been there, but I promise you it will end in tears. There's something behind those dashing looks and deep blue eyes that just isn't right and look what he did to poor Cath.'

'Mum, Cath is and always will be a bully. I have no sympathy for her.'

'Okay, I see that we are not going to get anywhere with this.' The emotional brick wall is back in place yet again. Her mum gets up. 'I'm going to bed, see you in the morning.'

Jade sits in silence, processing everything that has happened over the past few days. The deep sensual connection that she and Brax shared is special and she can't just erase it. Thinking about it is stirring up desires that are hard to suppress. She may not have known him long but the connection is strong. Why does it have to be so hard for her to find love?

At that moment a pebble strikes the window. *Strange.* Jade goes outside to investigate and finds Brax there.

'What are you doing here?'

'I needed to see you.'

'It's not a good idea for you to be here right now.'

'I had to see if you are okay. You left in such a rush and your mum said...'

'Wait, you came here today? After I left you? What did she say?'

'That you didn't want to see me ever again.'

'She did, did she?'

'Yes, but I just wanted to be sure before I move on.'

'Sarah is in hospital. She nearly lost her baby, well she did lose a baby but there's another one… Brax, it's all my fault. I don't…'

He crushes her against his chest, cutting off her words and all else but the sense of being in his arms, feeling their two hearts beating as one.

'Everything will be okay, babe,' he whispers. 'It's not your fault.' He lowers his head and claims her lips. The kiss is electrifying, her need to be with him all embracing.

A twig snapping spoils the moment.

Jade pulls away, breathing raggedly. 'Oh shit. Sean.'

'That jerk.'

'Wait here, I'll get rid of him.' Moving quickly, she leaves the shelter of the bushes. She needs to catch him before he knocks on the front door.

'Sean, what a surprise. Flowers? For my mum?'

'Were you in the bushes?'

'Thought I heard a cat.' She drags her fingers through her tangled curls. No leaves, thank goodness. 'So how are you, Sean?'

'I would be better if you'd agree to go on a date with me.'

'I'll consider it. Talk to me tomorrow.' Anything to get rid of him.

'I knew you wouldn't be able to resist my charm. It was just a matter of time. How about we don't wait till tomorrow. It's not late.'

'Uh – it's been a long day and I need to get to bed.' Oops. Wrong thing to say.

'Are you sure you don't want some company?' He shoots his eyebrows up and down suggestively.

'Sean.'

'Well you can't blame a guy for trying.'

He places the flowers by the front door. Jade makes her way down the drive. He grabs her bottom as she passes and gives it a squeeze.

'Sean, don't do that,' she snaps.

His tone is wheedling. 'Aw come on, you know that we make sweet music together.'

'We are dance partners and that's all it will ever be.' There. She's said it. And not for the first time. Maybe now he'll get the message and go. Just leave her alone. She turns to walk away.

Without warning he is grabbing her by the throat, pushing her back against the ground, shaking her.

'What's wrong with you? I have girls falling head over heels to go out with me and you…you just tease me.'

He pins her tighter and begins to tug at her trousers. His body is weighing her down. She can hardly move. His fingers are pressing into her throat, cutting off her breath. Fear is an icy chill that causes beads of sweat to break out on her face and arms.

Suddenly Sean's weight is lifted from her and he is being dragged into the bushes. She rolls onto her side, taking in great gulps of air, sobs of relief racking her body.

She's conscious of crashes, grunts, groans and thuds coming from behind the bushes but seems incapable of moving to find out what is happening there. Everything seems to be fading in and out. The front door bursts open. Her mum is there.

Then she's yelling, 'Get off him, you animal!'

It's the last thing Jade hears before she sinks into blackness..

She wakes in a hospital room to see her Mum sitting reading in the corner.

'Mum.' Her throat feels raw. It's hard to speak.

'Oh darling… you're awake.'

'What happened?'

'Don't you worry, love, that monster won't harm you again.'

Tears fill Jade's eyes and spill down her cheeks. She makes no move to dry them. 'I was so scared, Mum.'

'He's locked up now and can't harm you.'

'That's good.' Jade sags back against the pillows and closes her eyes. She's safe.

Shortly afterwards there is a tap on the door. Her eyes flick open and she freezes in shock at the sight of her visitor.

'Come in, Sean love, how are you?'

Jade turns away and curls into herself. What is he doing here? Isn't he in jail? Why is Mum being nice to him?

'Can I talk with Jade on my own please, Mrs McKenzie?'

'Eleanor please, and of course.' She bends to kiss Jade on the top of the head. 'I'll be back soon.'

Sean walks round and sits on the side of the bed where she can see him. She begins to whimper. He leans in close. 'Now we don't want to be making a fuss over what happened last night, do we, Jade?' She shakes her head in compliance.

'Good. We both know that it was a misunderstanding. We still have to dance together and we don't want to make the front page of the newspapers for the wrong reasons, do we?'

He is covered in cuts and bruises and he has a black eye. Jade looks away. It's all wrong. Brax saved her. And he's the one in jail?

Her mum returns and instantly picks up on the intense atmosphere. 'Sorry to disturb you two but it's important that Jade gets her rest now, Sean.'

'See you tomorrow, Jade.'

She makes no response.

'Goodbye, Mrs…Eleanor.' He kisses her on the cheek as he leaves.

She straightens Jade's bedcovers. 'What's going on with you two lovebirds?'

'Mum, where's Brax?'

'My love, he won't hurt you again. He won't hurt anyone. He's in custody.'

No! Every cell of her body is crying out in protest. How could they get it so wrong? She needs to put it right. *Think, think, think!*

It's hard to keep her voice steady as she suggests, 'Mum, I'm okay now for a bit if you want to get home for a while.'

'Well I suppose that I could go get a few supplies in before you come home. I want to spoil my girl.'

It feels like an eternity before she is gone and Jade is free to act. Brax is her hero and everyone is going to know it. She's going to make sure of it if it's the last thing she does.

Her body protests as she scrambles out of bed and quickly dresses, but she ignores the pain. Brax's wellbeing is more important than her own.

The door opens and she freezes.

'What are you doing?'

'Oh Sarah, I so need to see you right now.' Tears flow down her cheeks and she throws her arms around her friend in a welcoming hug.

'Your mum told me what happened. It was such a shock. Are you okay?'

'Mum's got it all wrong. Brax didn't attack me. He saved me from Sean.'

'You have to tell the police it was Sean.'

'He's threatened me.'

'Of course he has, he wouldn't want this coming out, his career would be over.'

'Brax was helping me, Sarah, and now I need to help him. I have to get him released. He can't be blamed for something he didn't do. It's all my fault he's in this mess. Oh, Sarah.' He voice breaks on a sob. 'I think I love him. Is've never felt like this about anyone before.'

Sarah brushes Jade's hair back off her face and says softly, 'I can see it in your eyes.'

'What will I do?'

'Jade McKenzie, you will follow your heart. For once in your life would you listen to it?'

'Really?'

'Yes, really, and don't worry about your mum, I will call her today. I've nothing much better to do lying up in a hospital bed for the next week.'

'Sarah, I love you.'

'What are you waiting for? Go get your hero.'

Jade sneaks past reception and out of the hospital and hails the first taxi she sees.

'Police station, please.'

'Wow, love, you must be having a bad day.'

Jade hasn't seen a mirror since the attack. She can only imagine how she looks, considering how bruised and battered her body feels.

'It's going to get better.' Jade's voice is firm. 'I'm on a mission to bail out my hero.'

The driver reaches into the glove compartment and hands her a silk bag containing makeup and a hairbrush.

'Here, love. Do yourself proud. We can't have you not looking your best for this big moment, now can we?'

When they arrive at the station, he brushes aside her attempt to pay for the fare and instead hands her his card. 'Just ask for Kev when you're ready to go home.'

'Thank you.'

'Good luck, young lady.'

Jade's legs don't seem to be working properly as she heads into the police station. Her heart is drumming an urgent beat in her chest.

'How can I assist you, ma'am?' asks the officer on the front desk. His eyes are tired, as if he's seen it all.

'You have a man in custody who is wrongly accused.'

'Oh really now, who might that be then?'

'Brax…Braxton.'

'Do we have a surname at all?'

Jade's heart sinks. Now that's a question. She has no idea.

'I am not sure, but he is Australian.'

'Ah yes, that one.'

'Yes, he has been wrongly accused.'

'He has, has he? And you have evidence to substantiate that?'

'I do. How do I get him released?'

'It's not that easy, young lady. Take a seat and I'll arrange for someone to interview you and take your statement, Miss–'

'Jade McKenzie.'

It feels like eternity before a female officer calls her name and ushers her into an interview room to take her statement.

She reminds Jade of her mum, direct but firm. 'So this is in the case of Braxton Hodgenson?'

'Yes. You see he didn't hurt me, he helped me. He's my hero.'

'All right. I need you to take me through the events of that night. Everything you can remember, even if you think it might not be important. Take your time, Jade.

Jade recounts what happens and the officer records it.

'We were to visit you in hospital today.'

'Yes, I guess so. Can I see Brax now?'

'I'm afraid not.'

'But I need to see him to tell him I love him.'

'Listen, love, your boyfriend has been accused of two serious crimes. For a start, we will need to compare your statements and take another statement from the person who alleges he was assaulted while coming to your defence. It won't happen in a hurry. I will keep you notified about what's happening.'

'Thank you.'

Heavy with disappointment, Jade leaves the police station and phones Kev to pick her up.

'It will turn out okay, love, you just need to be patient.'

She wishes she could be so optimistic.

'It's just me, Kev. I am a disaster when it comes to love.'

'Surely not, a real beauty like you would have the guys falling head over heels.'

'Not the right guys.'

She stares unseeingly through the taxi window, her focus instead on reliving every moment she spent with Brax. This can't be the end for them. It has to be the beginning.

Her phone rings. It's the constable who interviewed her.

'Hello, Jade, you'll be pleased to know that all charges have been dropped against Braxton and he will be released shortly.'

'Oh thank you, thank you, thank you. I'm on my way.' The words tumble over each other.

'Kev, turn around, they're letting him go.' She is practically bouncing off the seat in excitement.

Kev laughs. 'I've always wanted to do this.' He does a quick U-turn and speeds off on the way to unite two forbidden lovers, only slowing down once they reach the police station.

'Good luck, young lady.'

'Will you wait for us?'

His phone rings and he winks. 'Hello, Speedy Cabs at your service. Sorry, I have a booking.'

Jade dashes into the station, so excited she can barely contain herself. A few minutes later she emerges from the station, defeat in her hunched shoulders and lagging footsteps. Kev's arms are resting on the top of the taxi.

'No luck then?'

She sighs and lowers her head. 'No, it's just not meant to be.'

Kev opens the door for her and as she bends to climb in a thrill runs through her body.

'Hello, princess.'

'How —?'

Her question is halted by a searing kiss.

'My hero.' She says at last and sinks back against the seat.

Kev slips into the front of the car and coughs a little to grab their attention.

'Where to?'

'Crom Castle, we're going to make a dream come true.'

'What?'

'You told me you've always wanted to spend a night in a castle. Well I want to be the one who gives you that memory. Is that okay?'

'That's very okay.'

'We'll work it all out from there.'

'That sounds like a plan.'

As Brax claims her lips once more, Jade thrills to the realisation that the future is full of possibility. Others might consider them a mismatch, see their love as forbidden. But when you honour your heart's desire, it can only lead to your destiny. Fail to listen and you will never know the possibilities. Her heart is open. She's more than ready for what lies ahead for her and Brax.

Karen Weaver

Karen is a heart writer who embraces the beauty in every day and hopes to share that with others through her writing.

She embraced her passion for writing when she moved from Ireland to Australia in 2008.

Her writing has grown to have a deep connection link between Ireland, a heart centred place of magical beauty, and Australia, a place of wonder and opportunity.

Karen writes romance, spiritual and self-help as Karen Weaver, and children's books under the name Mamma Macs.

She has a diploma in humanities and with a background of tutoring drama she hopes to continue to be a positive part of people's lives.

As a busy mum of 6 and founder of Serenity Press she lives by the quote *Where there is a will there is always a way*. You can find Karen on her Facebook pages or www.serenitypress.org

www.ingramcontent.com/pod-product-compliance
Lightning Source LLC
Chambersburg PA
CBHW050502110726
47899CB00003B/1041